When Custard was grounded

D1393341

GO TEAM

www.roobarbandcustard.tv © 1974-2009 A&B TV limited. All rights reserved. Roobarb & Custard created by Grange Calveley.

© Mogzilla 2009 www.mogzilla.co.uk/roobarbandcustard ISBN: 978-1-906132-10-1. Printed in Malta. 5 4 3 2 1

Roobarb was walking in his garden.

Overhead, big jets scribbled vapour trails all over a sunny sky.

'It's perfect flying weather,'
thought Roobarb.

In his shed, Roobarb remembered the magnificent model aeroplane he'd made a few weeks earlier.

Roobarb thought and thought, until he *landed* on an idea.

Just then, Custard strolled in.

'Custard! I've decided to hold a model aeroplane show!'

'You what?' muttered Custard.
'Model planes doing aerobatics and tricks.
All flying by remote control,' explained Roobarb.

'Interested?' asked Roobarb.
'Not really,' scoffed Custard.
'There'll be a prize,' said Roobarb
enthusiastically,

'A spectacular trophy, that's
really a scrumptious golden sponge cake!'

'Golden sponge cake!' purred Custard, licking his lips as he scuttled off out of the shed.

Roobarb called all his friends on the Bone-Fone and invited them to his amazing air show.

As Roobarb's alarm clock barked four o'clock, the garden buzzed with aeroplane chatter like:

'Nice plane, Rabbit!' said Roobarb,
in a high-altitude kind of way.

'Ah, Mole! Love the headlight!
Blinding, what?'

'I say, Rooky. A red racer! Jolly
good luck in the show!'

Meanwhile, Custard was doing a dodgy deal with some bovver birds.
Their leader was called Feather.

'You know what to do?' Custard whispered.

'Yeah,' snorted Feather as Custard put an aeroplane disguise over the bird's head.

'Oi! Feather! No hopping! Remember, you're supposed to be a plane!' hissed Custard hoarsely, as Feather lined up with the model planes.

'Gentlemen, start your engines!' barked Roobarb. And the race began with a bang.

Then the tricks began.

They looped-the-loop.

They swooped down low.

They flew upside down.

They amazed the crowd with all manner of clever stunts.

Everyone clapped and cheered as they flew past.

But plane one was better than all the others.

Custard's *swooping* and *soaring* plane out-flew the rest!

As Custard pretended to fly his plane, he licked his lips.

The scrumptious golden sponge cake would soon be his!

'I declare this aeroplane show over!' announced Roobarb.
All the competitors flew their planes back and landed...

Some landed better than others.

When Feather landed, it was perfect.
Thinking he was sure to win, Custard grinned a greedy grin as

everyone went wild.

'Jolly good show everyone!' Roobarb waved to the crowd, 'Let's hear it for our amazing model makers with their

magnificent flying machines!'

'I'm your judge and I announce the winner is your friend and mine...'

But just as Roobarb was about to declare Custard the winner, Rabbit hopped over.

'Look!' said Rabbit, 'Custard's plane is eating the trophy!'

Roobarb spotted Feather pecking at the

scrumptious golden sponge cake!

'You there! You're a bird!' shouted Roobarb, 'You're supposed to be a plane! That's cheating, you stinker!'

Roobarb rescued the trophy from a flapping Feather.
Then he gave what was left to the real winner - Rabbit.

'Time to fly!' cackled Custard. But before he could escape, Roobarb spotted him.

'Hey you!' called Roobarb.
'You can forget about flying. From now on,

you're grounded!'

More marvellous adventures with Roobarb & Custard!

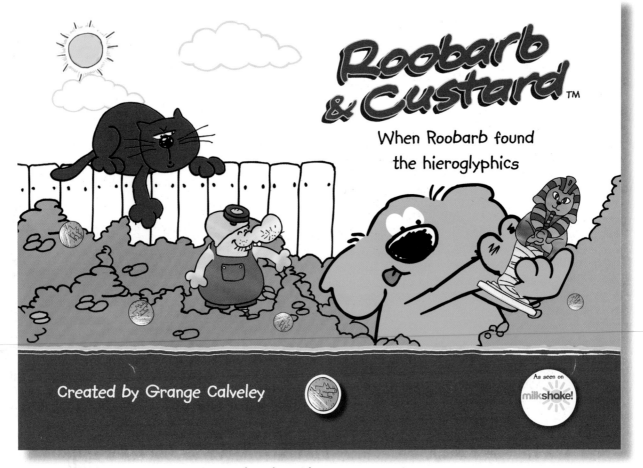

Roobarb & Custard™

When Roobarb found the hieroglyphics

Created by Grange Calveley

As seen on milkshake!

Join in the fun at
www.roobarbandcustard.tv

Roobarb & Custard™

When there was a pottery party

Created by Grange Calveley

Bag yourself more Roobarb & Custard books online at

www.mogzilla.co.uk/shop